KU-734-128

WOMBAT
STEW

MARCIA K. VAUGHAN

PAMELA LOFTS

A Scholastic Press book from Scholastic Australia

For Mum and Dad with love

Scholastic Press
345 Pacific Highway
Lindfield NSW 2070
An imprint of Scholastic Australia Pty Limited (ABN 11 000 614 577)
PO Box 579
Gosford NSW 2250
www.scholastic.com.au

Part of the Scholastic Group
Sydney • Auckland • New York • Toronto • London • Mexico City
• New Delhi • Hong Kong • Buenos Aires • Puerto Rico

First published by Scholastic Australia in 1984.
This edition published in 2017.
Text copyright © Marcia Vaughan, 1984.
Illustrations copyright © Pamela Lofts, 1984.

All rights reserved. No part of this publication may be reproduced or transmitted in any form or by any
means, electronic or mechanical, including photocopying, recording, storage in an information retrieval
system, or otherwise, without the prior written permission of the publisher, unless specifically permitted
under the Australian Copyright Act 1968 as amended.

National Library of Australia Cataloguing-in-Publication entry
Author: Vaughan, Marcia K. (Marcia Kay), author.
Title: Wombat stew / Marcia K Vaughan; illustrated by Pamela Lofts.
Edition: 30th anniversary edition.
ISBN: 9330303003035
Target Audience: For pre-school age.
Subjects: Animals--Australia--Juvenile fiction.
Wombats--Juvenile fiction.
Dingo--Juvenile fiction.
Other Authors/Contributors: Lofts, Pamela, illustrator.
Dewey Number: A823.3d

Typeset in Kitsu XD and Push Ups.

Printed in China by RR Donnelley.

Scholastic Australia's policy, in association with RR Donnelley, is to use papers that are renewable and made
efficiently from wood grown in responsibly managed forests, so as to minimise its environmental footprint.

10 9 8 7 6 5 4 3 2   18 19 20 21 / 1

One day, on the banks of a billabong,
a very clever dingo caught a wombat . . .

and decided to make . . .

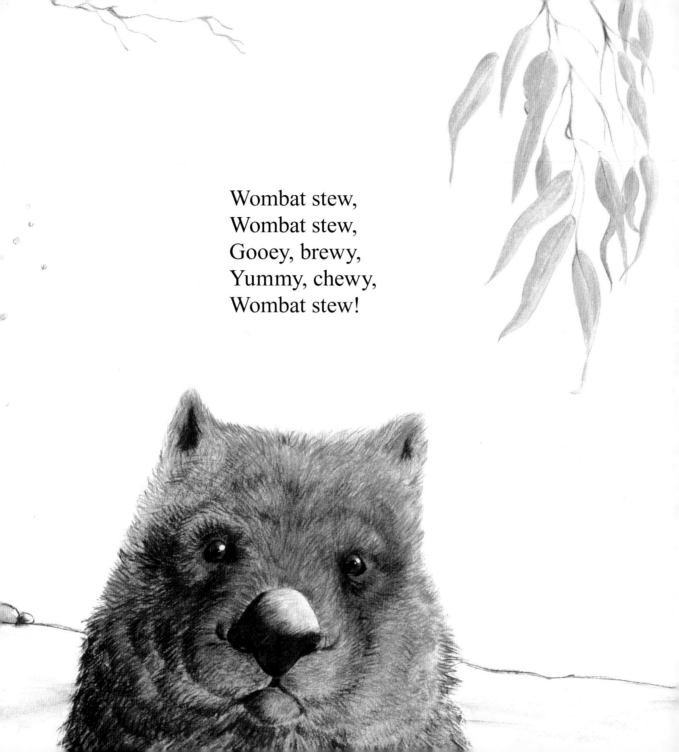

Wombat stew,
Wombat stew,
Gooey, brewy,
Yummy, chewy,
Wombat stew!

Platypus came ambling up the bank.

'Good day, Dingo,' he said,
snapping his bill.
'What is all that water for?'

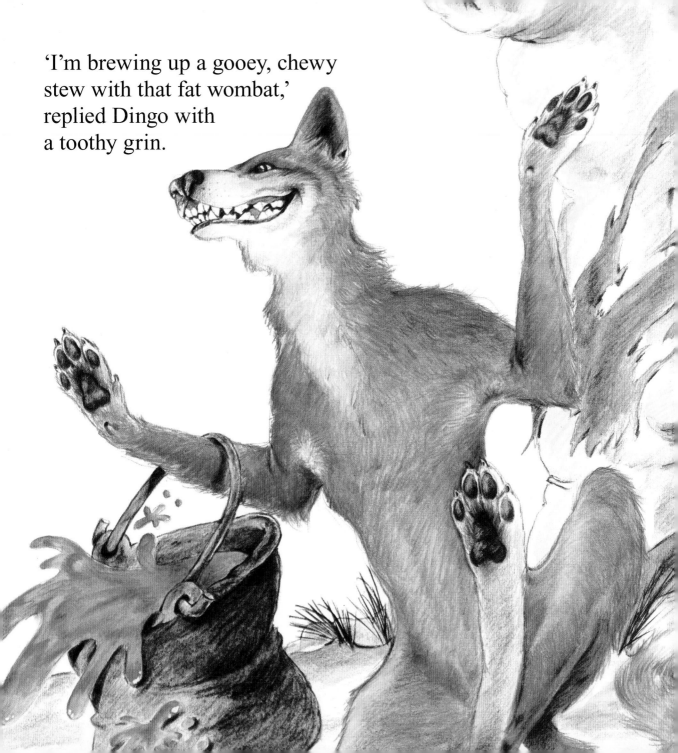

'I'm brewing up a gooey, chewy stew with that fat wombat,' replied Dingo with a toothy grin.

'If you ask me,' said Platypus,
'the best thing for a gooey
stew is mud. Big blops of
billabong mud.'

'Blops of mud?'
Dingo laughed.

'What a good idea.
Righto, in they go!'

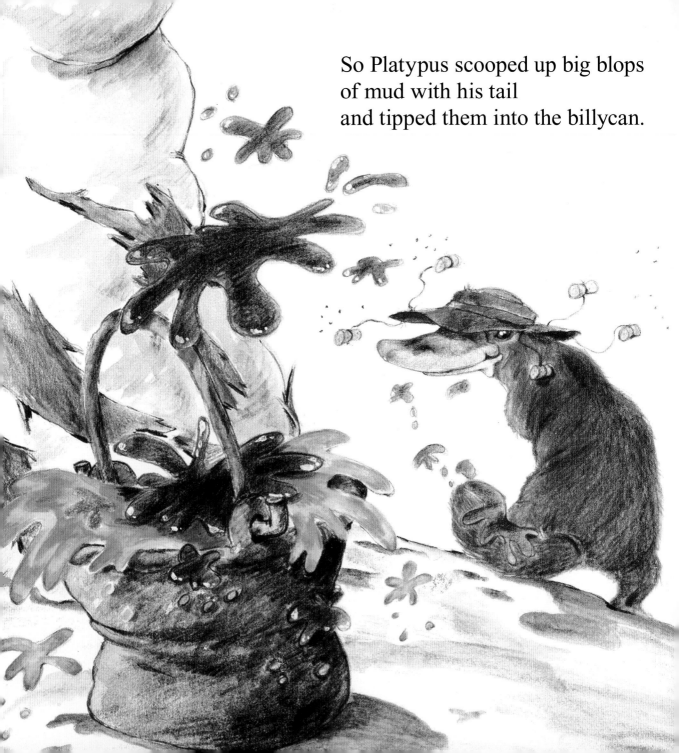

So Platypus scooped up big blops
of mud with his tail
and tipped them into the billycan.

Around the bubbling billy,
Dingo danced and sang . . .

'Wombat stew,
Wombat stew,
Gooey, brewy,
Yummy, chewy,
Wombat stew!'

Waltzing out
from the shade of the
ironbarks came Emu.
She arched her graceful neck
over the brew.

'Oh ho, Dingo,' she fluttered.
'What have we here?'

'Gooey, chewy wombat stew,'
boasted Dingo.

'If only it were a bit more chewy,'
she sighed. 'But don't worry.
A few feathers will set it right.'

'Feathers?' Dingo smiled.
'That would be chewy!
Righto, in they go!'

So into the gooey brew
Emu dropped
her finest feathers.

Around
 and around
the bubbling billy,
Dingo danced and sang . . .

'Wombat stew,
Wombat stew,
Crunchy, munchy,
For my lunchy,
Wombat stew!'

Old Blue Tongue the Lizard
came sliding off his sun-soaked stone.

'*Sss*illy Dingo,' he hissed.
'There are no fliesss in this ssstew.
Can't be wombat *sss*tew
without crunchy fliesss in it.'
And he stuck out
his bright blue tongue.

'There's a lot to be said for flies,'
agreed Dingo, rubbing his paws together.

'Righto, in they go!'

So Lizard snapped one hundred flies
from the air with his long tongue and
flipped them into the gooey, chewy stew.

Around
   and around
      and around
the bubbling billy,
Dingo danced and sang . . .

'Wombat stew,
Wombat stew,
Crunchy, munchy,
For my lunchy,
Wombat stew!'

Up through the red dust popped Echidna.

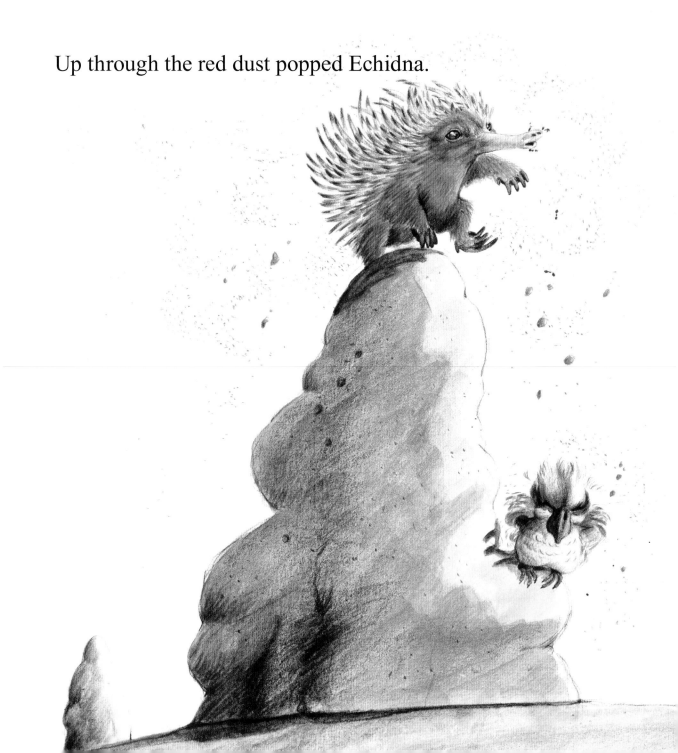

'Wait a bit. Not so fast,' he bristled,
shaking the red dust from his quills.
'Now, I've been listening
to all this advice –
and take it from me,
for a munchy stew
you need slugs and bugs
and creepy crawlies.'

Dingo wagged his tail.

'Why, I should have thought of that. Righto, in they go!'

So Echidna dug up all sorts of creepy crawlies
and dropped them into the gooey,
chewy, crunchy stew.

The very clever Dingo
stirred and stirred,
all the while singing . . .

'Wombat stew,
Wombat stew,
Hot and spicy,
Oh so nicey,
Wombat stew!'

Just then the sleepy-eyed Koala
climbed down the scribbly gumtree.

'Look here,' he yawned,
'any bush cook knows
you can't make a spicy stew
without gumnuts.'

'Leave it to a koala to think of gumnuts,'
Dingo laughed and licked his whiskers.

'Righto, in they go!'

And into the gooey, chewy, crunchy,
munchy stew
Koala shook lots and lots of gumnuts.

'Ah ha!' cried Dingo.
'Now my stew is missing only one thing.'

'What's that?' asked the animals.

'That fat wombat!'

'Wait!'

'Stop!'

'Hang on, Dingo!
You can't put
that wombat into
the stew yet.'

'Why not?'

'You haven't tasted it.'

'Righto! I'll taste it!'

And that very clever dingo
bent over the billy
and took a great, big slurp of stew.

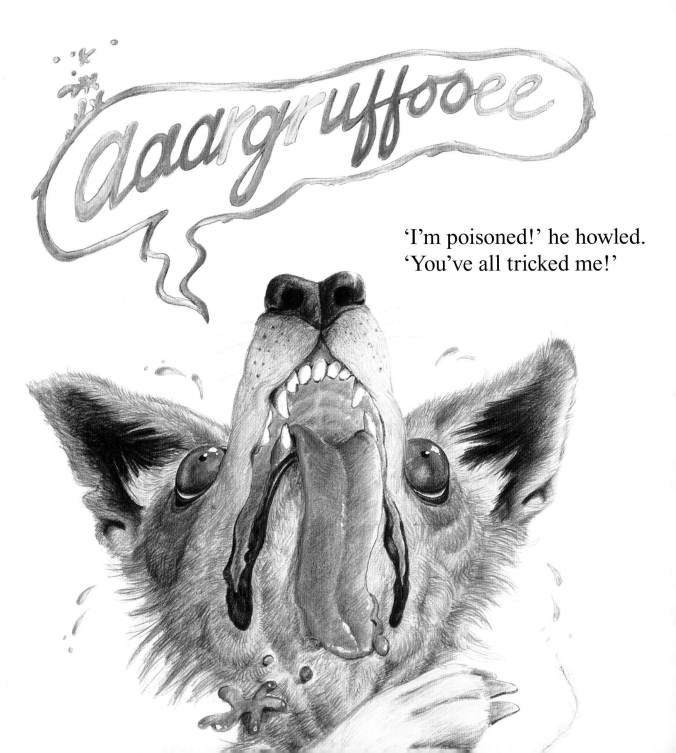

'I'm poisoned!' he howled.
'You've all tricked me!'

And he dashed away
deep into the bush,
never again to sing . . .

Wom-bat stew, Wom-bat stew,

Goo-ey, brew-y, Yum-my, chew-y, Wom-bat stew!

'Wombat stew,
Wombat stew,
Gooey, brewy,
Yummy, chewy,
Wombat stew!'